Published by Scholastic Inc.
90 Old Sherman Turnpike, Danbury, Connecticut 06816.

For information regarding permission, write to:
Disney Licensed Publishing
114 Fifth Avenue, New York, New York 10011.

ISBN 0-7172-6804-7

Designed and produced by Bill SMITH STUDIO.

Printed in the U.S.A.
First printing, September 2003

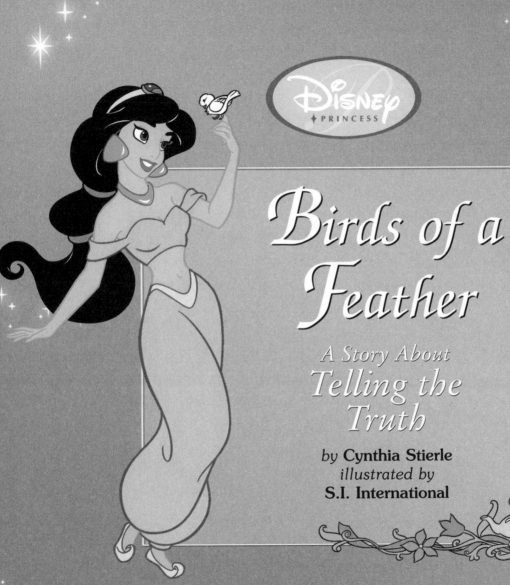

Birds of a Feather

A Story About Telling the Truth

by **Cynthia Stierle**
illustrated by
S.I. International

SCHOLASTIC INC.

New York   Toronto   London   Auckland   Sydney
Mexico City   New Delhi   Hong Kong   Buenos Aires

Jasmine watched the merchant in the purple robe bow to her father, the Sultan.

"Thank you for the gifts," the Sultan told the man. "I hope you enjoy your stay in Agrabah."

"Ah, but Your Majesty, we have one more gift for you." The man stepped aside. Behind him was a large object covered with a purple cloth.

"Oh, I love surprises," the Sultan exclaimed, clapping his hands together. He pulled off the cloth to reveal a golden birdcage with a beautiful bird inside.

The Sultan was astonished. "Why, this is a most wonderful gift," he said.

"Yes," agreed Jasmine, looking into the bird's large black eyes. Jasmine felt as if the bird wanted to talk to her.

The merchant smiled. "These birds are rare in my country, and few are ever captured."

Jasmine reached inside the cage to touch the bird. "Does it sing?" she asked.

The merchant shook his head. "It is said that the song of these birds brings happiness to all who hear it. But I must tell you the truth, Princess. I have never heard this bird sing."

Soon the merchant left. The Sultan smiled at the bird. He loved his new pet.

"Hmm," he murmured. "Perhaps if this bird likes living in the palace, it will sing for us." He looked at the bird. "We will give you nothing but the finest foods and care," the Sultan promised.

*J*ust then Aladdin noticed Abu. "Have you been eating the Sultan's gifts, Abu?"

Abu shook his head while hiding an orange behind his back.

"No fibs," Aladdin reminded his friend. "I'm sorry Abu ate the fruit, Your Highness," he added, apologizing to the Sultan.

"Oh, that's quite all right," the Sultan said. "But I do think your friend needs a bath." A bath! Abu didn't like that idea! He tried to escape by jumping on the Sultan's head. But the Magic Carpet caught him.

"Abu!" the Sultan said, wiping fruit juice from his face. Then he laughed. "Now we both need a bath!"

Jasmine watched everyone leave. She turned back to the beautiful bird. "It's the strangest thing," she said to the bird. "I feel as if you want to say something."

She paused, wishing the bird could answer. But it was silent.

"*I* hope Father is right," Jasmine told the bird. "I hope you like living in the palace with us." Then the princess left, leaving the bird alone.

*D*ays passed. The Sultan was true to his word and tried to make the bird happy.

The bird was given the finest foods.

The best musicians gave a concert for the bird.

$\mathcal{T}$he Sultan even took the bird to the camel races.

$\mathcal{B}$ut the bird never sang. Worse, its beautiful
tail feathers started to fall out.

"I wonder if this bird is sick," the worried Sultan
said one day. "Perhaps the air is too warm."

Jasmine shook her head. "I don't think that's it."

Aladdin frowned. "I wonder if there's a book that would tell us more about this bird."

"Wonderful idea, my boy!" exclaimed the Sultan. "Let's go to the palace library. There must be some way to help the poor creature." The two hurried off.

Jasmine stood quietly and looked at the bird. Suddenly she knew what was wrong. Just as she had once felt trapped behind the palace walls, the bird felt trapped in its cage.

"You need to be free, don't you?" Jasmine said to the bird. She opened the door of the cage. "I hope you can be happy at last."

For the first time, the bird's eyes sparkled. Then it quickly flew out of the cage.

"Father will be so happy to hear the bird isn't sick," Jasmine said, as she watched the bird soar into the sky. "I hope he's still in the library. I must tell him the good news."

She rushed out of the room to find the Sultan.

She had no sooner left the room when Abu wandered in. The playful monkey spied the open cage door and began to swing on it.

Just then Aladdin and the Sultan returned.

"Oh no!" cried the Sultan. "Abu has let my bird escape."

The little monkey's chattering echoed through the halls.

"What's wrong?" Jasmine cried, running up to them. "Father, I've been looking for you. I—"

"Not now, my dear," said the Sultan. "Now, Abu, I'm sure you didn't mean to let my bird out. If a *person* had done this, of course, I'd be furious." The Sultan sighed. "Please try to be more careful in the future."

"Come on, Abu," said Aladdin firmly, carrying the monkey out. "We need to go and have a chat about manners."

Jasmine looked at her father. Abu wasn't really in trouble. But if she told her father the truth, Jasmine knew she might be.

What would a princess do?

"*F*ather," began Jasmine. "What is it, my dear?" he answered in a hollow voice. He walked slowly over to his throne and sat down.

*J*asmine took a deep breath. "Abu wasn't the one who freed the bird. I did," she said softly.

"You?" the Sultan asked. His eyes widened. "My own daughter." His eyes filled with tears.

"*I* know how much you cared about the bird," Jasmine said. "But I realized the bird wasn't sick. It was unhappy living in a cage. It needed to be free."

Jasmine knelt next to the Sultan. "I know that you are angry with me. I'm sorry."

The Sultan was quiet for a few minutes. Jasmine's heart beat fast as she waited for her father's reaction.

Finally, the Sultan walked over and stroked Jasmine's head. "Ah, my child, I am not angry with you. I am proud of you."

Jasmine looked up, surprised.

"*I*t took courage to tell me the truth. And you are right. I want what is best for the bird," the Sultan sighed.

"Oh, Father," Jasmine cried, leaping up and giving the Sultan a hug.

"Now, I think I should find Abu and apologize," added the Sultan.

But then Aladdin and Abu came flying in on the Magic Carpet. "Jasmine! Your Majesty! You've got to hear—I mean, see this!" Aladdin shouted.

The Magic Carpet whisked them off to the royal garden.

*T*here, at the top of a tall tree sat the Sultan's bird, looking happier than anyone could imagine. Its wings were outstretched, and its song filled the air.

Jasmine listened to its music. "It does fill my heart with happiness," she sighed dreamily.

The Sultan squeezed Jasmine's hand. "Then it seems you both have the same talent," he said proudly.

The End